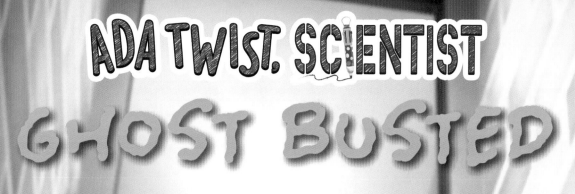

ADA TWIST, SCIENTIST
GHOST BUSTED

By Gabrielle Meyer

Abrams Books for Young Readers • New York

Ada, Iggy, and Rosie are having a sleepover at Iggy's dad's house for the first time ever, and Iggy wants to make sure it's a night they'll never forget.

"My dad used to have the most epic sleepovers here when he was a kid," explains Iggy.

"That's right," his dad says. "My friends and I would play Ping-Pong, eat yummy snacks, and tell spoooooky stories."

"Um, I don't think we'll get any sleep if we tell spooky stories," Iggy says. "And sleep is a pretty big part of a sleepover. It's in the name."

Iggy's dad chuckles. "Good point. We'll save the scary stories for another time. Have a fun sleepover, kiddos!"

After his dad leaves, Iggy asks his friends, "So what fun sleepover stuff should we do?"

"Why don't we do something your dad and his friends used to do?" suggests Ada. "Like play Ping-Pong!"

Iggy shakes his head. "Nope. No way. No Ping-Pong."

Ada and Rosie are confused. Why doesn't Iggy want to play Ping-Pong?

"Dad's old Ping-Pong table is in the basement," Iggy says with a nervous gulp. "And the basement is . . . haunted!"

Rosie is thrilled. "YES! I've always wanted to meet a ghost! Best sleepover ever!"

Ada has tons of questions for Iggy. "What does the ghost look like? What's its name? Did you talk to it? Can it float through walls?"

Iggy can't answer any of these questions, though, since he hasn't exactly talked to the ghost . . . or seen it. He's never even gone down to the basement because it's too spooky.

"Then how do you know there's a ghost down there?" asks Ada.

"Well, sometimes when I'm walking past the basement door, the lights flicker on and off and I hear a scary voice say, 'HOWLER'S HUNGRY!'"
"The ghost's name is Howler?!" asks Rosie. "Cute!"

"Hmm," says Ada. "Seems like we don't have enough evidence to say the basement is haunted . . . *yet.*"

And so the friends realize that's what they can do for their sleepover: Find out if there's a ghost in the basement!

Ada gets excited. "Looks like it's time to haunt our brains with ideas . . . in a brainstorm!" She taps her pen to her chin as she thinks. "Hmm. Oh, I know! We should invite another ghost over to see if there's already a ghost in the basement."

"But then there would be two ghosts!" says Iggy. "That's twice as scary!"

"True," says Rosie. "And they might not get along. Trust me, you don't want ghost drama in your house."

Rosie thinks they should make goggles that would help them see ghosts. "But I'm pretty sure we need purple space gas to make ghost goggles, so we'd have to travel through the galaxy to find some."

"I think our sleepover would be over by the time we got back," says Iggy.

Iggy proposes a new idea. "What if we design a ghost sucker-upper that can trap ghosts?"

Rosie doesn't like this idea, though, because it could hurt the ghost.

Iggy didn't think about that. "You're right. I don't want to hurt anyone, even a ghost."

Since they didn't come up with any good ideas in their brainstorm, Ada says they should use the scientific method!

First, they need to start with their question: Is the basement haunted? Then, they'll do background research, form a hypothesis, and test with experiments.

Luckily, Rosie has done tons of ghost research. She explains that according to spooky legends, ghosts make the temperature really cold, show up in photos as balls of white light, and cause electricity to go bonkers.

"And if you smell something weird, there's probably a ghost around," she adds.

Ada thinks they have their hypothesis: There's a ghost in the basement! Now they need to test with *experiments* to see if their hypothesis is correct.

"If we build a device based on what we know about ghosts, then we'll be able to collect evidence and see if there's one in the basement or not!" suggests Ada.

Even Iggy likes this idea. "Yeah! We can call the device the Spooky Scanner!"

In the lab, the three scientists build their Spooky Scanner with a thermometer to see if the air gets cold, a baby monitor to listen for weird noises, and a camera to take a picture of the ghost.

"Now we just have to put the Spooky Scanner in the basement so we can start collecting evidence," says Ada.

They make their way down to the basement, which is dark and creepy. Iggy doesn't like this one bit!

Suddenly, the lights flicker on and off and a deep voice roars, "HOWLER'S HUNGRY!"

Iggy screams and bumps into something in the dark. CRASH! "Ahh! I'm out of here!" he cries, then sprints back up the stairs.

Rosie and Ada set the Spooky Scanner down and

Once they're safe at the top of the stairs, Iggy says, "See? I told you it's haunted!"

"That was definitely spooky," agrees Ada. "But we still don't have enough evidence to prove there's a ghost."

Just then, the baby monitor makes a crackling noise, and they hear, "HOWLER'S HUNGRY!"

"Oh no!" squeals Iggy. "I'm too young to be ghost grub!"

Ada quickly clicks the remote so the Spooky Scanner will take a photo in the basement. "Smile for the camera, Howler!"

They return to the basement to collect their evidence, even though they're all a little scared.

"The basement is a lot colder now," says Ada through chattering teeth.

Rosie checks the thermometer on the Spooky Scanner. "Yup, it's definitely ghostly cold down here!"

Next, they check the camera. It took a photo of a ball of white light!
"Just like a ghost!" gasps Ada.

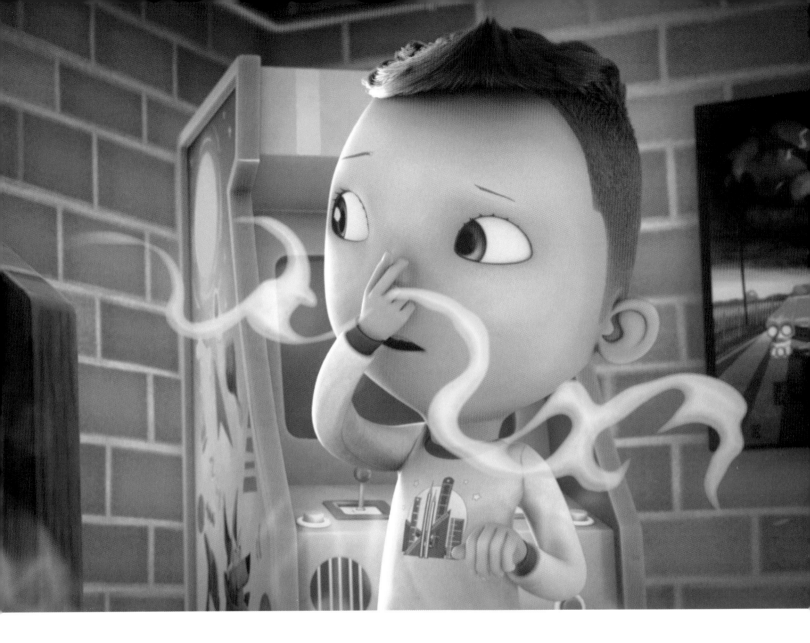

Iggy notices something else weird. "What's that smell? It smells like . . .
garlic."

    Wait a minute . . . the temperature is cold, the camera took a photo
of a ball of white light, the electricity is going bonkers, and there are
weird smells? Looks like they proved their hypothesis. There IS a ghost
down here!

Suddenly, the lights flicker on and off and they hear a loud *HOOOOOWL*.

The kids scream and sprint upstairs, where they bump into Iggy's dad.

"What's the matter, kiddos?" he asks.

Ada, Iggy, and Rosie explain that the basement is haunted.

"The ghost's name is Howler!" says Rosie.

"Howler, huh?" Iggy's dad says. "Wow, that must've been really spooky, but I think I have an explanation for everything, and it doesn't involve a ghost. Come with me." The kids follow him back down into the dark, cold basement.

"There's a bad fuse down here," says Iggy's dad. "That's why the electricity has been acting wacky." He tinkers with the fuse box, and the lights turn on.

Ada, Iggy, and Rosie look around the bright space—there's nothing spooky about this basement at all! In fact, it's the coolest basement they've ever seen. It has a TV, lots of books, an old-school arcade game, and a huge Ping-Pong table!

"My friends and I used to love playing all the games down here," says Iggy's dad. "Like this one. It's called, 'Howler's Hungry.'"

Ada, Iggy, and Rosie share a surprised look. *Ohh*. The scary voice they heard wasn't a ghost—it was an arcade game!

They take a closer look around the basement and see ice cubes spilling out of an open cooler on the floor.

"Oops," says Iggy with a laugh. "I think I accidentally knocked this over when I got scared. That's why it was so cold down here." He picks up something that fell out of the cooler—a clove of garlic! "*Aha*! The source of the garlic smell was . . . just garlic."

Ada realizes the camera took a picture of a Ping-Pong ball, not a ghost. "Looks like the basement isn't haunted, after all!" she declares.

"Yeah, there's no ghost down here," says Rosie. "Some of the evidence just made it *look* like there was."

"I've got a new theory," says Ada. "The Ghost in the Basement Theory: Gathering bits of evidence without looking at the whole picture can lead to false conclusions."

"Well, even though I didn't get to meet a ghost, this is still the best sleepover ever," says Rosie.

Iggy agrees. "Our first sleepover in this house has been pretty epic. And now I'm not afraid of the basement!"

Suddenly, the arcade game roars, "HOWLER'S HUNGRY!"

Iggy jumps, startled, then giggles. "I'll, uh, get used to that eventually." Everyone laughs with him. This really has been a sleepover they'll never forget!

Library of Congress Control Number 2022932923

ISBN 978-1-4197-6080-8

ADA TWIST ™/© Netflix. Used with permission.
Ada Twist, Scientist and the Questioneers created by Andrea Beaty and David Roberts
Book design by Charice Silverman and Brann Garvey

Published in 2022 by Abrams Books for Young Readers, an imprint of ABRAMS. All rights reserved. No portion of this book may be reproduced, stored in a retrieval system, or transmitted in any form or by any means, mechanical, electronic, photocopying, recording, or otherwise, without written permission from the publisher.

Printed and bound in U.S.A.
10 9 8 7 6 5 4 3 2 1

ABRAMS The Art of Books
195 Broadway, New York, NY 10007
abramsbooks.com